Roxie the Baking Fairy

ORCHARD BOOKS
338 Euston Road, London NW1 3BH
Orchard Books Australia
Level 17/207 Kent Street, Sydney, NSW 2000
A Paperback Original

First published in 2014 by Orchard Books

A CIP catalogue record for this book is available
from the British Library.

ISBN 978 1 40833 153 8

1 3 5 7 9 10 8 6 4 2

Printed in Great Britain

Orchard Books is a division of Hachette Children's Books,
an Hachette UK company

www.hachette.co.uk

Roxie the Baking Fairy

by Daisy Meadows

ORCHARD

www.rainbowmagic.co.uk

The Fairyland Palace
Sara Sketchley's house
Bridge
Maze
Rainspell Island
Park
Carys's Jewellery Shop
Beach and Promenade

Jack Frost's Ice Castle
Campsite
Girls' tent
Market Square
Mimosa Cottage
Pottery Hall
Sunshine Cake Shoppe
Polly Painterly's Workshop

Jack Frost's Spell

I'm a wonderful painter, you must have heard of me,
Marvel at my amazing artistic ability!
With palette, brush and paints in hand,
I'll be the most famous artist in the land!

The Magical Crafts Fairies can't stop me,
I'll steal their magic and then you'll see
That everyone, whatever the cost,
Will want a painting by Jack Frost!

Contents

Exhibition Day	9
The Great Bake-Off Disaster!	19
Star Shapes	27
Goblins at Sea	37
Fairy Crafts	51
And the Winner Is...	65

Exhibition Day

"I'm really sad it's the last day of our holiday," Kirsty sighed, placing a pile of folded T-shirts in her suitcase. "But I'm super excited about the Crafts Week exhibition and competition!"

"So am I," Rachel agreed. The girls were in Kirsty's attic bedroom at the B & B, packing their things ready to go home that evening. They'd spent

their week's holiday on Rainspell Island staying one night at the B & B with Mr and Mrs Tate, and the next at the campsite with Rachel's parents.

"It's been brilliant fun having a go at all the different crafts, hasn't it?" said Kirsty enthusiastically, and Rachel nodded. It was Crafts Week on Rainspell, and for the past six days the girls had attended various workshops. Today there was an exhibition of the best crafts produced during the week, and prizes would be awarded.

"And isn't it great that we *both* have entries in the exhibition, Kirsty?" Rachel said, stuffing socks into her suitcase. "I think your painting of me under a rainbow should definitely win a prize."

"No, I think *your* story about us

meeting the Rainbow Fairies on our first visit to Rainspell ought to win," Kirsty laughed. "And, of course, no one except us knows that it's all true!"

At that moment Mrs Tate came in. "Girls, have you finished your packing yet?" she asked.

"Just about, Mum," Kirsty replied, slipping her washbag into her case. "Can we take our entries to Artie for the exhibition now?" Artie Johnson was the organiser of the Rainspell Crafts Week.

"And then we're helping to bake cakes and cookies to serve at the exhibition this afternoon," Rachel added.

"I'll look forward to tasting them!" Mrs Tate said with a smile. "Off you go, then, and we'll see you at the exhibition later."

Calling goodbye to Mr Tate, the girls scooted out of the B & B. Rachel had the notebook that author Poppy Fields had given her at the story-writing workshop, and Kirsty had her painting tucked under her arm.

A large marquee had been set up on the promenade for the exhibition. The girls slipped inside and found Artie Johnson and her helpers setting up tables.

"Hello, girls," Artie said, beaming at them. "Do you have something for me?"

Rachel and Kirsty handed over the notebook and painting.

"Good luck in the competition," Artie told them. "What are you doing until then?"

"We're going to the Sunshine Cake Shoppe," Rachel explained. "We're helping to bake for the exhibition."

"My husband Ben is the head baker there," Artie said, eyes twinkling. "I'm sure he'll be delighted to have some extra pairs of hands!"

After saying goodbye to Artie, the girls

left the marquee and walked back along the promenade to the high street.

"The exhibition is going to be so much fun!" Rachel said excitedly.

"As long as Jack Frost doesn't ruin everything," Kirsty replied with a sigh.

Jack Frost had been up to his old tricks again. When Rachel and Kirsty arrived on Rainspell, they'd been invited to Fairyland by Kayla the Pottery Fairy, one of the seven Magical Crafts Fairies. The girls had been excited to discover that not only was it Crafts Week on Rainspell, it was also Magical Crafts

Week in Fairyland. Kayla had explained that King Oberon and Queen Titania would be choosing the most gorgeous fairy crafts to decorate their royal palace.

But before Magical Crafts Week could get under way, Jack Frost and his goblins had lobbed paint-filled balloons into the crowd. Green paint had splattered everywhere, and in the uproar, Jack Frost had snatched the Magical Crafts Fairies' special objects. Determined to be the best artist ever, Jack Frost had spun his icy magic and whisked himself, his goblins and the magical objects away to hide in the human world. The girls knew how important it was for the Magical Crafts Fairies to make sure that both humans and fairies had lots of fun

doing arts and crafts. But without their magical objects, the fairies were almost powerless. So Rachel and Kirsty had set themselves the task of finding all the magical objects, with the fairies' help.

"We mustn't let Jack Frost spoil the last day of Crafts Week. We *won't*," Rachel said firmly.

"There's one object left to find," Kirsty reminded her. She began to count them. "Kayla the Pottery Fairy, Annabelle the Drawing Fairy, Zadie the Sewing Fairy, Josie the Jewellery-Making Fairy, Violet the Painting Fairy, Libby the Story-Writing Fairy..." Then Kirsty gasped.

"Rachel!" she cried. "The last missing magical object must belong to Roxie the *Baking* Fairy!"

"Oh no!" Rachel groaned. "That

means the things we bake for the exhibition will be terrible – unless we can find Roxie's magical object before this afternoon!"

The Great Bake-Off Disaster!

A short while later, the girls arrived at the Sunshine Cake Shoppe at the other end of the high street. The windows of the bakery were filled with trays of cream cakes, fruit tarts, pretty little pastel-coloured cupcakes and chocolate brownies. Their mouths watering, Rachel and Kirsty went inside.

"Hello, girls, are you here to help with the baking for the exhibition?" a man in a white apron enquired, popping his head out of a door at the back of the shop.

"Yes, we are," Kirsty replied.

"Come and join us in the kitchen," the man said, smiling. "I'm Ben Johnson, Artie's husband."

The girls hurried into the kitchen. They were delighted to see some of the children who'd been at the workshops with them as well as the instructors, including author Poppy Fields, Polly Painterly the artist, Clayton Potts the potter and jewellery-maker Carys Silver.

Ben had already laid out flour, sugar, eggs and other ingredients on the worktops, along with bowls, wooden

spoons, scales and electric mixers. He handed out aprons, chefs' hats and different recipe cards. Rachel got lemon drizzle cake and Kirsty got sugar cookies.

"Right, everyone, as you know, we want some wonderful cakes and cookies for the Crafts Week finale this afternoon!" Ben said.

Everyone began gathering their ingredients. Rachel picked up an egg box, but she was dismayed when it slipped from her hands and all the eggs smashed into bits on the floor.

"What a butterfingers I am!" Rachel sighed.

"Don't worry," Ben said. "We have plenty more." But as he took some fresh eggs to Rachel, there was a shout from Polly Painterly who was making a banana and chocolate chip cake.

"Mind that banana skin on the floor!" she exclaimed.

She was too late. Ben skidded on the banana skin and knocked Carys Silver's bowl of coffee-and-walnut cake mixture onto the floor. Then one of the children dropped a bag of icing sugar. The box hit the floor and the icing sugar billowed out in a white, misty cloud. Everyone started coughing.

"Oh no!" Kirsty suddenly exclaimed in horror. "I should have put a teaspoon of salt and two-hundred-and-fifty grams of sugar in my cookie dough – but I switched them round! I'll have to throw this salty mixture away."

"This is all because Roxie the Baking Fairy doesn't have her magical object!" Rachel whispered.

Ben helped Carys clear up the mess and then they started the cake again. But when Ben switched on the electric mixer to beat the butter and sugar with the flour and eggs, he gave a shout of dismay as the mixture flew *everywhere*.

People ducked as it splattered the worktops, the windows and even the ceiling.

"This kitchen is a disaster zone!" Rachel groaned, wiping a splash of cake mix off her nose. She picked up her mixing bowl, and, to her amazement, out fluttered Roxie the Baking Fairy, shaking icing sugar from her wings!

Star Shapes

"Hello, girls," Roxie murmured. She looked very pretty in her candy-pink, full-skirted dress with a ruffled petticoat peeking out and pink ballerina flats decorated with tiny gold star shapes. "I'm sure you've been expecting me. This kitchen is in chaos!"

"You can say that again, Roxie!" Rachel whispered as a smell of burning filled the air.

"My peanut cookies!" one of the children yelled. Ben dashed over to an oven and pulled the door open. Smoke poured out as he removed a tray of burnt cookies, and everyone else gathered around to look.

"Girls, will you help me get my magical star-shaped cookie-cutter back?" Roxie said urgently while everyone was distracted. "Those naughty goblins must be around here somewhere."

"Of course we will," Kirsty replied.

Flashing the girls a grateful smile, Roxie dived inside Kirsty's apron pocket.

"We've got to find the cookie-cutter, and *fast*," Rachel told Kirsty. "Otherwise there'll be no cakes or cookies for the exhibition this afternoon."

"Well, this looks wonderful!" Ben said suddenly from the other side of the kitchen.

Curious, Rachel and Kirsty turned to see what he was talking about. He was admiring a cake made by some children wearing bright green aprons and matching chefs' hats.

"What an amazing cake!" Poppy Fields exclaimed, as everyone went to look.

"Wow!" Kirsty murmured to Rachel. "It really *is* spectacular!"

The enormous cake had been decorated to look like the Rainspell seaside. There was an ocean of blue icing swirls, golden sands of buttercream icing sparkling with edible glitter and white marzipan cliffs.

"There's even a model of my lighthouse!" Polly Painterly laughed. "And it's got all the right colours, too."

"See the surfers on the sea?" said Ben, pointing to a couple of tiny green figures on top of the blue icing waves. "And the boat? This really is a magnificent cake! How on earth did you manage to bake it and decorate it so quickly?"

"Because we're baking masterchefs, that's why!" one of the children retorted, and the others chuckled.

"This cake will be perfect for the exhibition," Ben told them. "You can take it over to the marquee."

Proudly the group of children carried the cake away. But as they passed the girls, Rachel noticed long green noses poking out from underneath their chefs' hats. She glanced at Kirsty.

"Goblin alert!" Rachel whispered.

The goblins were muttering to each other and Rachel moved a little closer to catch what they were saying.

"We're not sharing this cake," the biggest goblin said. "No way!"

"Let's take it to the beach and eat it ourselves!" a goblin with

huge ears suggested. The others chortled with glee.

"Let's follow them, Kirsty," Rachel said urgently. Immediately the girls went over to Ben.

"We're just going out to get some ideas for decorating our cakes," Kirsty told him.

"That's fine," Ben agreed.

Quickly Rachel and Kirsty took off their aprons and hats and Roxie hid herself in the pocket of Rachel's shorts. Then they followed the goblins out of the shop. They were just in time to see them heading down the steps to the beach.

"We could keep up with the goblins more easily if we could fly," Rachel began, and right on cue, Roxie fluttered out of her pocket.

"Just what I was thinking, girls!" Roxie cried, her eyes dancing.

Rachel and Kirsty ducked down behind the harbour wall while Roxie worked her magic. In a trice the girls became fairy-sized, with sparkling wings on their shoulders. Then the three of them whizzed along the beach until they caught up with the goblins.

"Stay high above their heads so they don't spot us," Roxie whispered.

From overhead, the girls and Roxie had a better view of the wonderful cake below them. Suddenly Roxie gasped aloud.

"Girls, the goblins have used my magical cookie-cutter to make lots of shapes for their cake!" she declared with a frown. "See the tiny star on the sail of the boat? And on the flag stuck in the sandcastle?"

"I can see another." Kirsty pointed down at the cake. "It looks like a starfish half-buried in the sand."

Roxie peered down. "That's no starfish," she announced, "that's my magical cookie-cutter! Girls, we must get it back! Any ideas?"

Goblins at Sea

The goblins placed the cake carefully on a flat rock on the beach, then stood back to admire it.

"I'll eat the lighthouse," the biggest goblin declared.

"I want that bit!" another goblin grumbled.

"I'll eat the ocean," announced the goblin with the huge ears.

"That's not fair," the goblin next to him complained. "It's almost half of the cake!"

"So?" the big-eared goblin retorted with a shrug.

All the goblins began squabbling loudly over which part of the cake they wanted for themselves.

"Now's our chance, girls," Roxie whispered. "Let's try and dig my magical cookie-cutter out of the icing sugar!"

Roxie, Rachel and Kirsty flew down to the cake, keeping out of the goblins' sight. The goblins were bawling and shrieking at each other, and there was a lot of pushing and shoving going on.

Now that they were close to the cake, Rachel could see a very faint golden haze of magic around the top of the cookie-cutter. "There's just enough sticking out for us to grab hold of," Rachel murmured. "If we all pull together–"

But suddenly Rachel broke off in alarm. A big green goblin hand was sneakily reaching for a chunk of cake right next to where the three of them were hovering. Instantly Roxie pulled the girls away to hide in a cave cut in the side of the marzipan cliffs.

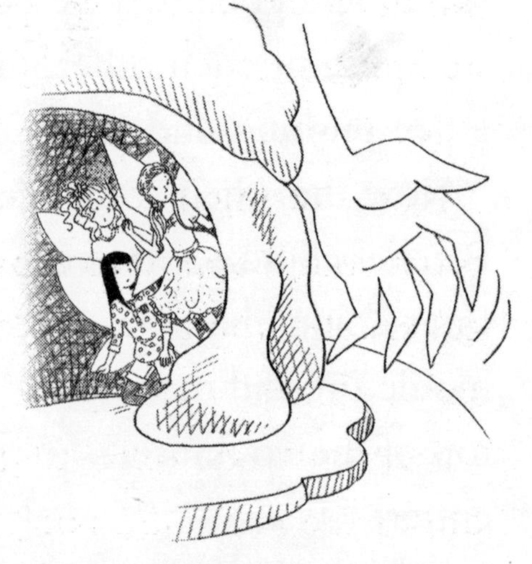

"Stop that!" the big goblin yelled at the cake thief, suddenly spotting what he was up to.

"But I want some cake!" the goblin muttered sulkily.

As the goblins continued to argue, Rachel turned to Kirsty and Roxie.

"I've thought of a way to get the magical cookie-cutter back," Rachel whispered. "But Kirsty and I need to be our normal size, so first we need to escape from this cave!"

Roxie grinned. "The goblins are practically coming to blows over the cake," she pointed out. "So I think it's safe to leave!"

Swiftly Roxie and the girls whizzed out of the cave and back to the harbour wall. The goblins never noticed a thing. Then a burst of glittery magic from Roxie's wand restored Rachel and Kirsty to their usual height. Rachel outlined her plan, and the three of them headed back

to the goblins once more, Roxie keeping out of sight high above the girls.

"Oh, what a fabulous cake!" Kirsty gasped. All the goblins turned to stare at her, which was just what Rachel was hoping for. It was Kirsty's job to keep the goblins distracted while *she* tried to grab the cookie-cutter. "Did you bake it?"

The goblins nodded proudly.

"It looks delicious," Kirsty said eagerly.

"Can I have a little taste?"

The goblins glared at her.

"No way!" screeched the biggest goblin. "This cake is for goblins only!"

"But it's nice to share," Kirsty told him.

"Goblins don't share," the goblin with the huge ears snapped. "Goblins are greedy!"

"*I'm* not greedy," another goblin protested crossly.

"Then give this pesky human girl *your* piece of cake!" retorted the big-eared goblin.

None of the goblins were looking at the cake so they didn't see Roxie hovering above it. Meanwhile, Rachel, keeping out of sight behind Kirsty, tried to prise the magical cookie-cutter out of the buttercream sand. But unfortunately for Rachel, the goblin who had attempted to steal some cake earlier decided to try his luck again while the others were arguing with Kirsty. Sneaking over to the cake, the goblin spotted Rachel and Roxie immediately, and gave an angry roar.

"Get away from our cake!" he yelled.

Furiously the other goblins hurried forward and snatched the cake from

under Rachel's nose. They scurried off across the beach, carrying the cake aloft.

"Look!" one of the goblins shouted, pointing at an inflatable boat drawn up onto the sand.

Quickly the goblins piled into the boat, taking the cake with them. The biggest goblin pushed the boat into the shallow waves, then jumped in himself.

"You can't catch us!" the goblins chanted smugly as they rowed away, leaving Kirsty, Rachel and Roxie on the beach. "And you're not getting any of

our cake, either!"

"What shall we do now?" Rachel asked, dismayed.

Helplessly Kirsty glanced around the beach for inspiration. Suddenly she spotted a seagull hopping across the sand. He looked rather familiar.

"Roxie, that's the seagull who helped us get Josie the Jewellery-Making Fairy's magical beaded ribbon back!" Kirsty explained quickly. "Could you ask him to fly after the goblins and pull the cookie-cutter out of the cake with his sharp beak?"

"That's a brilliant idea, Kirsty!" Roxie agreed. She flew over to the seagull and began whispering to him while the girls waited. The seagull cocked his head to one side, taking in everything Roxie

was saying and squawking a reply. Then, spreading his enormous white wings, he launched himself up into the air.

"The seagull says he remembers the naughty goblins, and he's glad to help," Roxie told the girls. "Let's hope this works!"

The seagull was already hovering above the goblins' boat as it bobbed up and down on the waves. As Roxie and the girls watched hopefully, the seagull swooped down, his dark eyes fixed on the cake.

The goblins shrieked with fear. "Go away, horrid bird!" the biggest goblin

yelled, trying to fend the seagull off.

"He's trying to eat our cake!" another goblin shrieked.

The seagull lunged for the cake as the goblins hit out, trying to frighten him off. The seagull tried again, but two of the goblins snatched the cake away from him just in time. The seagull missed the cake and instead his beak jabbed into the

side of the boat, puncturing it.

There was a loud hissing sound as the boat began to deflate.

"Oh no!" Rachel cried. "We've got to do something quickly, or the boat will sink!"

"Taking the cake, Roxie's magical cookie-cutter *and* the goblins with it!" Kirsty added.

Fairy Crafts

The goblins were beginning to panic.

"Our boat's sinking!" the biggest goblin shouted. "We'll have to swim for it!"

"Goblins can't swim!" another yelled. "And anyway, we can't leave the cake behind!"

"Roxie, we need a boat so we can row out and rescue the goblins," Rachel told the little fairy.

Roxie immediately waved her wand, conjuring up a cloud of fairy magic. When the sparkles faded away, another inflatable boat appeared on the beach. The girls pushed the boat into the shallow water, then jumped in and grabbed the oars. They began to row towards the goblins with Roxie flying overhead.

"Help!" the biggest goblin shrieked when he spotted the girls coming towards them. "We're going to drown!"

"No, you're not," Rachel said firmly. "We're going to save you. But first you must give Roxie her magical cookie-cutter back!"

The biggest goblin looked reluctant, but the others turned on him.

"Give it back!" they chorused.

The biggest goblin dug the cookie-cutter out of the icing sugar and held it up. With a cry of joy, Roxie swooped down to take possession of it. At the touch of her tiny fingers, the cookie-cutter shrank down to its fairy size.

Then the girls rowed closer so that the

goblins could scramble aboard their boat, bringing the cake with them.

"The icing's started to melt!" the big-eared goblin groaned miserably. "And the lighthouse and the surfers have fallen over."

"The cake is ruined!" grumbled the biggest goblin.

"But I bet it still tastes good," Kirsty reassured them.

Fluttering above them, Roxie used her

magic to divide the cake into slices, and they all had a piece as the girls rowed back to shore.

"Mm, it's yummy!" the goblins declared, their green faces sticky with icing. They were still munching away when the girls and Roxie left them on the beach and dashed back to the bakery, Roxie again hidden in the pocket of Rachel's shorts.

The kitchen was filled with the smell of baking when Rachel and Kirsty went in.

"Girls, we've been busy while you've been away!" Ben declared.

Rachel and Kirsty were delighted to see that the worktops were now covered with delicious-looking cakes and cookies.

Everything was going smoothly now that Roxie had her magic cookie-cutter back! Quickly the girls replaced their aprons and chefs' hats, Roxie taking her

place in Kirsty's apron pocket again, and then they set to work. Rachel made her lemon drizzle cake and Kirsty produced a tray of golden-brown sugar cookies. Then, with Roxie whispering helpful instructions, they made a big batch of cupcakes decorated with seaside-themed shapes – marzipan fish, seashells, lighthouses and even surfers.

"These are lovely, girls," Ben said when they'd finished. "I'll pack them up, ready for the exhibition."

Rachel and Kirsty took a quick look at the other cakes as Ben packed them away.

"This sandcastle-shaped cake is amazing!" Rachel marvelled. The cake had towers and turrets, just like a sandcastle, and it was covered in gold icing with a flag stuck in the top.

"Who made it?" Kirsty asked.

"I did," said one of the helpers, a girl called Anuoluwa. "Ben said I should enter it in the competition."

"Definitely – you ought to win a prize!" Kirsty told her.

As everyone took off their aprons, Roxie tugged at Kirsty's sleeve. "Are you coming to Fairyland to see the Magical Crafts Week exhibition?" she asked.

"We wouldn't miss it for anything!" Kirsty replied. Calling goodbye to Ben and the others, the girls hurried outside. Then Roxie's magic swept them all away to Fairyland.

The crafts exhibition was taking place in the Fairyland Palace and the room was packed with fairies, including King Oberon and Queen Titania, who were viewing the display of crafts. When Roxie, Rachel and Kirsty arrived, everyone cheered.

"Girls, you've saved our Crafts Week!" declared Kayla the Pottery Fairy.

"What good, true friends you are, girls," said Queen Titania with a sweet smile.

"Thanks to you, we have lots of entries for the competition," King Oberon added. "It's going to be very difficult to choose a winner."

Roxie, Kirsty and Rachel looked around the exhibition. There were lots of beautiful craft projects of all kinds. The Rainbow Fairies had entered colourful paintings and drawings.

The Fashion Fairies had designed and sewn a range of bright, glittering dresses while Hannah the Happy Ever After Fairy had written a brand-new fairytale.

As the king and queen discussed the entries they'd seen so far, Rachel and Kirsty saw Cherry the Cake Fairy rush in, followed by the Sweet Fairies. They were all carrying cakes on gold platters.

"Roxie got her magical cookie-cutter back just in time!" Cherry gasped. Her spectacular cake was shaped like the Fairyland Palace, complete with four pink towers made of icing.

"Otherwise our baking would have been a disaster," added Coco the Cupcake Fairy. She held a plate of cupcakes decorated with miniature fairies with glittery wings.

Suddenly a blast of cold air swirled around the room. Seconds later Jack Frost stalked in, the self-portrait he'd done at Polly Painterly's workshop tucked under his arm. He was also carrying a snowflake-shaped cake, a notebook, a necklace made of icicles, a sketch of his Ice Castle, a clay pot with a white glaze and a flowing, ice-blue cloak. "I'm entering all the categories!" Jack Frost said with a smug sneer. "My crafts are the best, so I'm bound to win first prize!"

And the Winner Is...

King Oberon stepped forward. "The queen and I are happy to announce the winner of Magical Crafts Week," he said. "First prize goes to Cherry the Cake Fairy for her wonderful cake!"

The fairies applauded but Jack Frost stamped his foot.

"NO!" he roared furiously. "What's the point of doing crafts if I don't win the competition?"

"The point is to have fun!" Rachel told him. "Did you enjoy doing your crafts?"

Jack Frost looked sulky. "Well... yes," he admitted reluctantly. "I especially liked painting my self-portrait."

"Taking part and having fun is very special," Kirsty said. "That's what really counts. Why don't you hang your self-portrait in your bedroom? Then you can look at it all the time!"

Jack Frost stroked his frozen beard thoughtfully. "Yes, I could do that," he said at last, his icy face breaking into a smile. Then he went off happily, back to his Ice Castle, taking his crafts with him.

"Girls, thank you a million times over

for your help!" Roxie said gratefully, giving them both a hug. "Magical Crafts Week really has been *magical* because of you. And now," Roxie went on, her eyes twinkling, "you have your very own exhibition to attend, so it's probably time you were going!"

The other fairies gathered around as Roxie prepared to send Rachel and Kirsty back to Rainspell with her magic.

"Congratulations, Cherry," Rachel

called. "Goodbye, everybody!"

"Well done, Cherry," Kirsty said. "See you all again soon!"

And then, with their fairy friends calling farewell, the girls were whisked away to Rainspell. In the blink of an eye, they found themselves next to the exhibition marquee.

"Here come our parents!" Rachel murmured, spotting her mum and dad and Mr and Mrs Tate walking down the promenade. "We're just in time."

"Hello, girls,"

called Kirsty's dad. "Can't wait to taste all the cakes you've been making!"

"Let's look at the exhibition first," Mrs Tate said with a smile.

Inside the marquee, all the best crafts from the week were on display. Kirsty's painting had been hung on a display board with other pictures, and Rachel's notebook had been left open on a table so that everyone could read her story. Anuoluwa's sandcastle cake was there too, as well as pencil sketches of

Rainspell, silver bracelets and earrings from the jewellery-making workshop, some glazed clay pots and sewing projects including a patchwork quilt of Rainspell Island.

After admiring the displays, the girls

and their parents joined the line of people queuing for refreshments.

"Girls, these cupcakes are delicious

and very moreish!" Mr Tate told them, taking a big bite.

Towards the end of the afternoon, Artie Johnson called for silence in the marquee so that she could announce the results of the competition.

"What a difficult but very enjoyable job our judges have had today," Artie said with a smile. "First prize goes to Anuoluwa Barker for her wonderful sandcastle cake!"

Beaming, Anuoluwa hurried forward to accept her prize, a set of craft books, while everyone applauded.

"Now we have a *joint* second prize to award," Artie continued. "But I know these two girls are great friends, so they won't mind sharing this lovely jewellery-making kit. Second prize goes to Kirsty

Tate for her painting *Rachel Under a Rainbow* and to Rachel Walker for her story *Rainbow Fairies*!"

Thrilled, the girls went up to receive their prizes.

"I hope all of you have enjoyed Crafts

Week," Artie said as the girls rejoined their parents. "I'm sure you've loved trying new crafts. And I've really enjoyed organising everything, too – it's been a magical week!"

Rachel and Kirsty glanced at each other and shared a secret smile. As Artie said, it really *had* been a magical week. And both girls silently hoped that there were a lot more magical adventures ahead with their fairy friends!

The End

Now it's time for Kirsty and Rachel to help...

Lila and Myla the Twins Fairies

Read on for a sneak peek...

"This is the house," said Rachel Walker, pointing up at a tall, white townhouse.

A bunch of pink balloons was tied to the gatepost, and there was another bunch pinned to the front door. Rachel smoothed down her party dress and smiled at her best friend, Kirsty Tate. Kirsty was staying with Rachel for the half-term holidays.

"It was really kind of your friends to invite me to their birthday parties," said Kirsty. "I've never been to two in one day before!"

Rachel's school friends Jessy and Amy

were twins, and they were having two separate birthday parties – one for each of them.

"Jessy and Amy's parents are really good fun," Rachel said as they walked up to the front door. "They're letting Jessy have her party this morning, and Amy have hers this afternoon."

Read Lila and Myla the Twins Fairies
to find out what adventures are in store for Kirsty and Rachel!

Meet the Magical Crafts Fairies

Jack Frost has stolen the Magical Crafts Fairies' special objects. Can Kirsty and Rachel help get them back before Rainspell Island's Crafts Week is ruined?

www.rainbowmagicbooks.co.uk

Competition!

The Magical Crafts Fairies have created a special competition just for you!
In the back of each book in the Magical Crafts series there will be a question for you to answer.
First you need to collect the answer from the back of each book in the series.
Once you have all the answers, take the first letter from each one and arrange them to spell a secret word!
When you have the answer, go online and enter!

What is the name of the Drawing Fairy in the Magical Crafts Fairies series?

_ _ _ _ _ _ _ _ _

We will put all the correct entries into a draw and select a winner to receive a special Rainbow Magic Goody Bag featuring lots of treats for you and your fairy friends.
You'll also star in a new Rainbow Magic story!

Enter online now at www.rainbowmagicbooks.co.uk

No purchase required. Only one entry per child. Two prize draws will take place on 29th August 2014 and 31st October 2014. Alternatively readers can send the answer on a postcard to:
Rainbow Magic, Magical Crafts Fairies Competition,
Orchard Books, 338 Euston Road, London, NW1 3BH. Australian readers can write to:
Rainbow Magic, Magical Crafts Fairies Competition, Hachette Children's Books,
level 17/207 Kent St, Sydney, NSW 2000. E-mail: childrens.books@hachette.com.au.
New Zealand readers should write to:
Rainbow Magic, Magical Crafts Fairies Competition,
PO Box 3255, Shortland St, Auckland 1140

Have you read them all?

The Rainbow Fairies

1. Ruby the Red Fairy ☐
2. Amber the Orange Fairy ☐
3. Saffron the Yellow Fairy ☐
4. Fern the Green Fairy ☐
5. Sky the Blue Fairy ☐
6. Izzy the Indigo Fairy ☐
7. Heather the Violet Fairy ☐

The Weather Fairies

8. Crystal the Snow Fairy ☐
9. Abigail the Breeze Fairy ☐
10. Pearl the Cloud Fairy ☐
11. Goldie the Sunshine Fairy ☐
12. Evie the Mist Fairy ☐
13. Storm the Lightning Fairy ☐
14. Hayley the Rain Fairy ☐

The Party Fairies

15. Cherry the Cake Fairy ☐
16. Melodie the Music Fairy ☐
17. Grace the Glitter Fairy ☐
18. Honey the Sweet Fairy ☐
19. Polly the Party Fun Fairy ☐
20. Phoebe the Fashion Fairy ☐
21. Jasmine the Present Fairy ☐

The Jewel Fairies

22. India the Moonstone Fairy ☐
23. Scarlett the Garnet Fairy ☐
24. Emily the Emerald Fairy ☐
25. Chloe the Topaz Fairy ☐
26. Amy the Amethyst Fairy ☐
27. Sophie the Sapphire Fairy ☐
28. Lucy the Diamond Fairy ☐

The Pet Keeper Fairies

29. Katie the Kitten Fairy ☐
30. Bella the Bunny Fairy ☐
31. Georgia the Guinea Pig Fairy ☐
32. Lauren the Puppy Fairy ☐
33. Harriet the Hamster Fairy ☐
34. Molly the Goldfish Fairy ☐
35. Penny the Pony Fairy ☐

The Fun Day Fairies

36. Megan the Monday Fairy ☐
37. Tallulah the Tuesday Fairy ☐
38. Willow the Wednesday Fairy ☐
39. Thea the Thursday Fairy ☐
40. Freya the Friday Fairy ☐
41. Sienna the Saturday Fairy ☐
42. Sarah the Sunday Fairy ☐

The Petal Fairies

43. Tia the Tulip Fairy ☐
44. Pippa the Poppy Fairy ☐
45. Louise the Lily Fairy ☐
46. Charlotte the Sunflower Fairy ☐
47. Olivia the Orchid Fairy ☐
48. Danielle the Daisy Fairy ☐
49. Ella the Rose Fairy ☐

The Dance Fairies

50. Bethany the Ballet Fairy ☐
51. Jade the Disco Fairy ☐
52. Rebecca the Rock'n'Roll Fairy ☐
53. Tasha the Tap Dance Fairy ☐
54. Jessica the Jazz Fairy ☐
55. Saskia the Salsa Fairy ☐
56. Imogen the Ice Dance Fairy ☐

The Sporty Fairies

57. Helena the Horseriding Fairy ☐
58. Francesca the Football Fairy ☐
59. Zoe the Skating Fairy ☐
60. Naomi the Netball Fairy ☐
61. Samantha the Swimming Fairy ☐
62. Alice the Tennis Fairy ☐
63. Gemma the Gymnastics Fairy ☐

The Music Fairies

64. Poppy the Piano Fairy ☐
65. Ellie the Guitar Fairy ☐
66. Fiona the Flute Fairy ☐
67. Danni the Drum Fairy ☐
68. Maya the Harp Fairy ☐
69. Victoria the Violin Fairy ☐
70. Sadie the Saxophone Fairy ☐

The Magical Animal Fairies

71. Ashley the Dragon Fairy ☐
72. Lara the Black Cat Fairy ☐
73. Erin the Firebird Fairy ☐
74. Rihanna the Seahorse Fairy ☐
75. Sophia the Snow Swan Fairy ☐
76. Leona the Unicorn Fairy ☐
77. Caitlin the Ice Bear Fairy ☐

The Green Fairies

78. Nicole the Beach Fairy ☐
79. Isabella the Air Fairy ☐
80. Edie the Garden Fairy ☐
81. Coral the Reef Fairy ☐
82. Lily the Rainforest Fairy ☐
83. Carrie the Snow Cap Fairy ☐
84. Milly the River Fairy ☐

The Ocean Fairies

85. Ally the Dolphin Fairy ☐
86. Amelie the Seal Fairy ☐
87. Pia the Penguin Fairy ☐
88. Tess the Sea Turtle Fairy ☐
89. Stephanie the Starfish Fairy ☐
90. Whitney the Whale Fairy ☐
91. Courtney the Clownfish Fairy ☐

The Twilight Fairies

92. Ava the Sunset Fairy ☐
93. Lexi the Firefly Fairy ☐
94. Zara the Starlight Fairy ☐
95. Morgan the Midnight Fairy ☐
96. Yasmin the Night Owl Fairy ☐
97. Maisie the Moonbeam Fairy ☐
98. Sabrina the Sweet Dreams Fairy ☐

The Showtime Fairies

99. Madison the Magic Show Fairy ☐
100. Leah the Theatre Fairy ☐
101. Alesha the Acrobat Fairy ☐
102. Darcey the Dance Diva Fairy ☐
103. Taylor the Talent Show Fairy ☐
104. Amelia the Singing Fairy ☐
105. Isla the Ice Star Fairy ☐

The Princess Fairies

106. Honor the Happy Days Fairy ☐
107. Demi the Dressing-Up Fairy ☐
108. Anya the Cuddly Creatures Fairy ☐
109. Elisa the Adventure Fairy ☐
110. Lizzie the Sweet Treats Fairy ☐
111. Maddie the Playtime Fairy ☐
112. Eva the Enchanted Ball Fairy ☐

The Pop Star Fairies

113. Jessie the Lyrics Fairy ☐
114. Adele the Singing Coach Fairy ☐
115. Vanessa the Dance Steps Fairy ☐
116. Miley the Stylist Fairy ☐
117. Frankie the Make-Up Fairy ☐
118. Rochelle the Star Spotter Fairy ☐
119. Una the Concert Fairy ☐

The Fashion Fairies

120. Miranda the Beauty Fairy ☐
121. Claudia the Accessories Fairy ☐
12.2. Tyra the Dress Designer Fairy ☐
123. Alexa the Fashion Reporter Fairy ☐
124. Matilda the Hair Stylist Fairy ☐
125. Brooke the Photographer Fairy ☐
126. Lola the Fashion Fairy ☐

The Sweet Fairies

127. Lottie the Lollipop Fairy ☐
128. Esme the Ice Cream Fairy ☐
129. Coco the Cupcake Fairy ☐
130. Clara the Chocolate Fairy ☐
131. Madeleine the Cookie Fairy ☐
132. Layla the Candyfloss Fairy ☐
133. Nina the Birthday Cake Fairy ☐

The Baby Animal Rescue Fairies

134. Mae the Panda Fairy ☐
135. Kitty the Tiger Fairy ☐
136. Mara the Meerkat Fairy ☐
137. Savannah the Zebra Fairy ☐
138. Kimberley the Koala Fairy ☐
139. Rosie the Honey Bear Fairy ☐
140. Anna the Arctic Fox Fairy ☐

The Magical Crafts Fairies

141. Kayla the Pottery Fairy ☐
142. Annabelle the Drawing Fairy ☐
143. Zadie the Sewing Fairy ☐
144. Josie the Jewellery-Making Fairy ☐
145. Violet the Painting Fairy ☐
146. Libby the Story-Writing Fairy ☐
147. Roxie the Baking Fairy ☐

There's a book of fairy fun for everyone!

www.rainbowmagicbooks.co.uk

Meet Lila and Myla the Twins Fairies!
Can the fairies stop Jack Frost before he uses
their magic to create his very own twin?